DON'T LEAVE ME

I NEED YOU

SAYAN BANIK

To my special one, wherever you are at the moment...

Contents

Foreword

"True love will triumph in the end - which may or may not be a lie, but if it is a lie, then it's the most beautiful lie we have."

—John Green

1

Who is she?

There are certain times in life when even the person of his choice goes to others without his knowledge. Sometimes he has to leave the place with a smile, perhaps for her good, or for the good of her family. And that's exactly what happened to me...

I just got up from class ten. And What happened to the stem tie! News pages, TVs, radios, mobiles, all places of warning— do not leave the house, stay at home. Stay healthy, be careful.

As my exams ended on February 27, I went to my aunt's house without a day's delay. My favourite cousin lives there, and I enjoy spending time with her. Anyway, at least I didn't go down without explaining myself first. Lest the bus-train all stop for the Chinese virus corona.

The exam is over, and the virus arrives. What a pity! I could not go anywhere outside, nor could I keep my feet outside the door. Whatever if I survive, I will be able to travel a lot.

Day by day the outside environment began to calm down. Roads are deserted, and there is not a single person in the market. All the shops are closed except the drug stores. The country's economy has also plummeted— street dogs and cats are starving to death. Fish-meat shops closed, sweet shops closed. The roar of wailing has risen from house to house. In the end, the government announced in seven days, that all that has to be done in the market between 7 & 10 in the morning is to do it again, again with a face mask with social distance.

As usual, the people followed the rules of the government— as soon as they broke the law, they started eating the sticks of the police. Leaving the house without any reason had to face various punishments from the administration. However, they were doing it for the protection of our people.

Gradually the lockdown came to an end. I got up at Eleven then. New school, new subject, new friend but I could not find any joy in it. I sat at home and took classes on my mobile. Meanwhile, many people in the country have become infected and are on the verge of death. Teachers are not teaching in the tuition that I will start. I bought a book at home and started reading. Then he called a few days later and said that he would start taking classes on WhatsApp.

The first day of eleven geography tuition. A notification was entered on my mobile, to join the group. By clicking on the invite link sent by Sir, I was added. I did not see anyone in group info in the same contact. Meanwhile, Sir continues to explain the topic of 'Recent Changes in Land Use in China'. All of a sudden, as if to say something, it was typed in a group in clear English,

"Agriculture is becoming a pasture in the pursuit of rapid economic development."

I saw, sir, typing— he wrote, "All right, Hiya."

Hiya...! There is something hidden in the name. Who is she? Which school does she go to?? Where does she live?

What does she look like?

At the end of the class, various questions started popping into my head. I opened her chat and saw that she was online. After a while, it went offline, and I realised that the last seen was off. I didn't know if it would be right to text Hiya. If she blocks me! I thought...

Thinking about all this, I saved her number and took it. I wrote 'Hiya' and saved it with two embarrassing emojis. But saving with emojis next to names like this, I've never been in save a contact with anyone before. Why am I ashamed or embarrassed, why did I save her name! I was confused at that time...

Even after saving the number, Her About, DP was not showing anything. Understood, Privacy has kept my contact. From time to time I would sit anywhere and open her chat and do some typing. But, because of some fear, I did not dare to message her.

The lockdown was slowly coming to an end, and people began to walk on the streets again, with no hope of opening an educational institution. Even then, people were getting infected— people on the streets, wearing masks again, began to walk with their protection. Offices and courts are often crowded all day long. People obeyed the rules of distance as much as possible.

It was during this time that I joined SFI through a movement at my former school. When people fall in love with a new person, just like they want to hold them with passion and love, just like when they see Subhash Basu's picture, the hairs on my body get excited. As soon as I entered that small office of the Students Federation of India, an emotion would come. Seeing Subhash Basu's big picture hanging, seeing Che Guevara's picture would have been a different feeling in my mind! I was thrilled to be

associated with a generation that has moved forward from the pages of the history of various revolutionaries.
I went to various processions and took to the streets to protest against rape. We were ready to do whatever it took to open the eyes of the government. If the real justice of that girl had been found in the street with a candle in hand for a while, this India would have been free from rape. Even today, I wish I could see a rape-free India. Where girls will not be disrespected, there will be no nude videos of girls on various social sites, they will be able to go out on the streets like men even at night and at noon...

Damn ashes! Why I sat down to write it all! Where despite the tears of the girls, day after day, the lap of the parents is empty. Justice there again! What will happen by writing this? Who will listen to the words of this small writer like me! Who can hear? No one can hear, no one. No one will be able to hear, the water of sorrow inside my mind. Where day after day one girl after another is being raped. Suck...!

2

She is Offline

Over time, that is likely to change...
I was forced to leave SFI. That I completely omitted is also not correct. Then I started reading different types of books. Starting from 'Netaji's Dream and Pursuit', 'In The Context of Marxism' etc. My curiosity about communism grew.

Meanwhile, Covid's situation became somewhat normal. My tuitions started fairly well. Geography sir said that he will not teach in the previous house, they have all taken science. So he asked me to come to study in a new place.

I took the bicycle out of the house at 8 AM on Monday. When I got there, I saw two boys' bicycles leaning side by side, and a lady's bicycle leaning forward a little. I leaned my bicycle beside the bicycle and entered to Room.

Sir was teaching seven students. I saw four girls and two boys sitting there.
Asked, "Ayan, did you buy the book I asked you to buy online?"
I said, "No sir. I have ordered, it will come in three or four days."
I went and sat next to the boys. Sir said again after a while, "Ayan, you go and sit next to her. Share her book and read

today." Sir pointed his finger at a girl.

I sat next to the girl wearing black jeans and a sleeveless T-shirt. I don't know, why I couldn't look at that girl's face. Just as there was fear when texting Hiya, that fear still worked.

I sat next to her and thought that girl might say something, but no. She put her book in the middle. She was holding a pen in his right hand and marking in the book. I was gradually moving from the book to her hand.

After a while, the book closed. I thought, maybe this time the defeat! The girl probably put the slap on my cheek! I sat down with my head down.

After a while, Sir said, "All right, Hiya, stay here till today."

I looked up and saw that we had finished reading. After talking to Sir, the girl also went out and I realised by now that the girl was no one else, that Hiya. The one I had been sitting next to for so long had become so inattentive, still, I was thinking about it. I went out and saw that Hiya was waiting for my bicycle to move. I looked at her and removed the bicycle and she took out her bicycle and went home.

There was great joy in my mind to see Hiya, to be able to sit next to Hiya and to be able to put my bicycle next to her bicycle. All this within these two hours, again without knowing it. Understood, everyone wants to find the opportunity to know - but, in finding something unknown, there is a hidden peace of destiny.

♡♡♡

I couldn't believe it, I just sat next to her. She looks so beautiful! Her big eyes, fair hands, her hair up to her back. With so many girls in the group, who knows why I saved her name Hiya that day! And that's probably why my attraction to her was growing.

When I came home, I kept thinking about her. I couldn't

figure out if it was okay to text her! As the days passed, the weeks began to pass. At the end of the week, one month went by and two months went by. I thought that this time I have to message Hiya, whatever. Otherwise, I will just keep thinking about her, and she will not even know me.

Within these two months, I typed a story into my mobile notepad. With the last two or three lines left, I completed them. I thought this is the story I send to Hiya. If she wants to read she will read, otherwise she will not read. At least I can say hi-hello...

As usual, I opened her chat and pasted the story. I saw that she was not online and then I send it.

After two or three minutes I saw that the story has become a seen. She was not doing an online show, last seen, DP could not be seen. Even after sending the story, at least she would reply by saying 'who are you, but she did not do that. I thought, fucking damned. Hiya may have blocked me after seeing such a message from an unknown number.

After four or five days, the mobile beeped. As soon as I open the phone, I see the message. I pulled out my teeth and went to one side of the room and saw:

"Is this your personal number?"

I wrote, "Yeah, why?"

Hiya said, "No, I just asked..."

When she asked me if it was my personal number, I said, "Save this number then!"

She told me, "I can't save your number... If my mom sees a boy's number on my phone... She will scold me..." sent me two sad emojis.

After a while, she told me, "The story is really beautiful..."

I said, "Finally you read it!? :)"

Hiya said, "Umm... How do you write so well?"

I was a little embarrassed and said, "Oh no-no!!! Where else can I write so beautifully!!!"
"Nopeee... When I read this today, I got into the story... And I was thinking, what a wonderful way to screw people over."

I sent her two more stories to impress Hiya. Hiya said she would read them later.

Since I first texted her on December 10, we haven't had a day off without talking. We used to talk every day, but when we had time, we would talk for hours on WhatsApp.

We still did not recognise ourselves as such. And even if I went to study on Monday, I wouldn't sit next to her, but every word she said, laughing and talking with her friends would have been captured in my ears. When I got home, I started talking to her and started taking my conversation forward. I would tell her everything from what I was doing to what I ate.

One day she sat down and asked me, "Hey? Why don't you talk to me about tuition? Even if you go out, leave immediately...???"

After a while, I saw her message and said,
"One day the time will come when I will talk to you all the time, not just in temporary tuition."

Hiya may not have understood the meaning of my words. Without saying anything else, she went offline.

3

Don't Marry The One You Love

I have talked to her for a while now and I have realized that she is a very intelligent girl. I sat down to write for the readers after getting a lot of evidence. That day when she disagreed to save my number on her mobile, I realized that Hiya is not a girl like that, she is different from everyone else. She excused her mother for not saving the number so that she would not have to ask for a change. Although her mom might check the phone, or why lie to me!

Anyway, at least I didn't go down without explaining myself first. But there was also a condition that she would 'Clear chat' after the talk. I fully agreed with that though.

Hiya is texting one Sunday afternoon, "If you don't talk to me tomorrow, I won't talk to you on WhatsApp..."

"Oh-oh!! No-no-no... It's a little scary to talk to you."

"Am I a ghost? If not... Why are you so afraid to talk? Where do you swear to the rest of the girls, except me!"

"You can talk to me too?" I deliberately changed Hiya.

"No...I mean... Wanna talk to you... But... You get out so fast..."

"Okay, I'll try to talk."
"Don't just try, you have to talk to me..."

I was lying in bed at night thinking of DP wearing her Saree. Although she looks beautiful in the picture, she looks even more beautiful from the front.
Can I talk to this beautiful girl tomorrow? What should I call it? What to say first?
Hi Hiya! Umm-no...
Hello Hiya! Umm-no-no...
Hiya yesterday you told me to talk, tell me what to say? Noooooo...

I fell asleep thinking about all this alone. I washed my eyes and face in the morning, put on my jacket and went to tuition. I came to tuition and saw that no one came. I left the bag inside and came out and stood on the road. After waiting for a long time, I saw Hiya coming here to talk to her friend. I straightened my hair with my hands, cleared my throat and said,
"Hey, Good morning!"
Hiya smiled with her clenched teeth and said, "Hey-hi! Good morning"
Her friend next to her stared at us, not understanding anything.

After tuition, I said, "You are going home alone! I also had a little work to be done there— But..."
Hiya said, "But what? Let's go... I also find it boring to go alone. If you go with me, you'll be my partner too."

Hiya left her bag on the bicycle basket and started cycling. I also continued to talk while riding my bicycle next to her.

"Then? Are you scared?" She looked at me temporarily and said.
I said, "If you stop talking on WhatsApp too! So I said out of

fear..."
Hiya looked at my face and smiled. I kept my smile to myself.

Straight road. The two of us have been cycling ever since. I realised that she came from far away and went to tuition. Without a word, she said,
"Any girlfriends?"
I immediately laughed and said, "Whose? Mine?"
"Yes, do you have?"
As soon as I said "yes..." hesitantly, her face turned pale.
I said again, "Yes! That was a long time ago."
"I was too in a relationship with a bad boy for 4 months. You know?"
"Sorry!"

"It's ok... Carry on"

"You know what, I don't understand relationships. If true love is born in someone, they can be laughing and playing in every moment of life. That person can be arrogant, can cry and even suffer. But if the other one doesn't smile, doesn't love him or her Actually, she doesn't understand the other one."

"Really!"
"So, don't always think of Rabindranath's quote, 'Don't Marry The One You Love.' Saying this, laughing... I left Hiya at her home and went home.

ÞÞÞ

It was not too late for me to realise that a little smile in life is a weapon in different situations. Even today, tears of joy come to my eyes when I think of the small smiles and the small joys that she has shared with me.

When it comes to writing the truth, readers may think that

the character of the writer is bad. If you think so, then you can skip reading this far.

There was a girl named Atasi. Her hair was short, her complexion was fair, and she always wore shorts that I never liked. Whatever it is, I've been in a relationship with Atasi for about a year and a half now. That girl almost always gave me different gifts she would take me on trips to different places, etc. She would do all the expenses.

But I do believe that a relationship between money and gifts cannot be maintained. If the two do not have the same mind, then it is better not to build that relationship. And that was never between us. I ended my lifelong relationship with her with a letter one day. And then, in my life, an innocent, polite, calm girl like Hiya appeared.

Ever since Hiya came into my mind, a lot of smiles have come into my life, and various troubles have also floated away like a cloud. The distance between some loves is so great, it takes a lot of hard work to get that loved one.

I went for a walk with my mother, I came to my aunt's house. I miss her so much. If I could bring her! Her mind was too bored, I came out.

At the end of five days, she started urging me to leave. I finally came home in seven days.

I was also happy to see the smile on her face. A girlfriend can do so much caring. But is she my girlfriend? Did Hiya's feelings come to me? —As soon as I talk to her, these two questions keep popping into my head all the time. If Hiya thinks of me as her best friend, does what we say happen to other best friends?

One day, on Monday, while walking down the street, Hiya asked,

"Who are you going to go to for Saraswati Pujo?"

"I didn't think it right! My friend, also said that he will hang

out with his girlfriend. What else can go around with him!"
"Huh! all my friends will hang out with their GF-BF too... Don't even take me." I could understand in the twist of her words that she was indirectly telling me the words to go with her to Saraswati Pujo.

I asked bluntly, "Will you go around together?"

Hiya may have been scared at first and said, "If no one in the house sees us, they will cut off my legs and hand it over."

I smiled.

Later she said to herself, "All right. But this time we will go together."

4

Her First Touch

Although there was Relation with me, it was all right! But, some things I did not let us come at all. What comes first to say, kisses. Yes, I tell you these because you can understand the whole thing well. It is understood that the first relationship is broken when a kiss or any physical relationship can be loved by the second one. Which I did not do with the burden— even did not hug. That is why it was probably the feeling of love to hide Hiya and could be born in myself.

Even if Atasi is in a relationship with me, all conversations can be okay. But, some things about me I did not let come. The first thing that comes to mind is a kiss. Yeah Al that sounds pretty crap to me, Looks like BT ain't for me either. How much it hurts to fall in love with a second person for a kiss or a physical relationship can be understood by breaking up the first relationship. Which I never did with Atasi— not even hug. And maybe that's why I hid Hiya and gave birth to the feeling of love in myself.

Saraswati Pujo. The sky has been cloudy since morning. I woke up in the morning and sent Hiya to 'Good Morning' message. I saw that the message showed Delivered. I thought she must have got up before me today. After a while, the reply came,

“When will you leave?”

“I'm going to take a bath now. Then I will go out after pujo. It may be about 11 o’clock.”

“I just took a bath. I am sitting with wet hair now. Dad will worship, then...”

Hiya is ‘Chatterjee’, Brahmin in caste. They no longer need a priest. Parents and uncles who have taken paita can hear the pujo by themselves by chanting a few Sanskrit mantras.

I said, “Okay, I’ll take a bath. Let me know before you leave the house.”

After taking a bath, with pujo, after eating and drinking, it was half past I got up. Hiya told me to come after a beautiful Punjabi. I took out an evenly folded Punjabi from the cupboard and put it on. As the pyjamas became smaller, I wear my jeans pant.

I have never met Hiya like this before. Today I am going to meet her for the first time. Feeling very nervous, inside myself. I texted and asked,

“Where are you??”

“I’m standing at the gate of the stadium,” Hiya said. “But I can’t, see you.”

I said, “Stay there, I’m coming.”

As soon as I entered the gate of the stadium, I saw her standing on the left side. She is wearing a red saree, lipstick on her lips, blushing powder on her cheeks, long heels on her feet, a purse in her hand and a mobile phone. It feels pretty good when girls wear saree. But I can’t say what I felt when I saw Hiya.

I saw two more girls standing next to her. Hiya went to introduce,
"She is my maternal sister, Risha."
I said "Hi" to Risha.
Hiya started saying again, "And she is..."
I interrupted her and said, "She is Fulmoni. I already have WhatsApp contact." They all started laughing.

I thought maybe Fulmoni came to see me like this. But what an irritation! This girl is holding us back. I turned to Hiya and said,
"Why has Fulmoni been hanging out with us ever since?"
Hiya came and said, "Damn! I don't understand either—now she's saying she's not hanging out with anyone, so she's with us..."
"What Fucking damned! ...So she's with us!" I punched my legs.

I asked, "Okay... Where are we going now?"
Risha said, "Ayanda, go to the park. It will be good there."
I said, "Damn! There is nothing like that. Do something, come and see the school-college pujas."
Hiya said, "Yeah-yeah! that's right..."

Risha doesn't agree at all, in the end, we have to go to the par,k. Meanwhile, another incident. We are all walking along the road, the throat of a girl I know from behind is floating in our ears. The throat seemed a little clearer,
"Hey, Dada! you're going to the,e park!" My sister has been watching from behind for so long.
I looked to the side and saw my mom walking with my sister too. I thought defeated. Did they have to come here today? I didn't understand whether I would laugh or cry, so I told my mother,
"Mom, look, I'm just... Hanging out with these girls..." After saying that, I saw the look on my mom's face and realised

that my mom could not understand in this crowd that I was hanging out with girls or someone else. But as soon as I said that, my mom understood and I said to my sister,
"Rumi, roam with mom, I'm going..." I got stuck in my stupid shame.

Anyway, at least I didn't go down without explaining myself first. Fulmoni has got a companion to go around. Meanwhile, Risha called her boyfriend and went to the other side. Hiya and I seem to be a little empty after so long. For a while, both of them were silent without getting any word. The conversation that we started later continued until we got home...
We ate Panipuri... Took selfies... After that, Hiya and her sister went home. And I came home too. I still remember that day we first met.

ÞÞÞ

Today I heard that her cousins have come to her house. She went to the station to bring her sisters.

Hiya kept telling me in the morning,
"My sisters are coming today, you know? It's even gone..."
"Wow, that's pretty good. Have fun these days!"
"Ummmmm!!"
"What did you say to your sister's name?"
"Rumi. Her name is Paramita Das. We all call her 'Rumidi'."

Today with Hiya, there was no word in all day! Now it seems to me that if I can't talk to her, even if I finish the whole day's work, it may be unfinished in some places...

It took five days. There was not much talk with Hiya. She is texting me one night,
"Wanna meet you tomorrow?"
I paused and said, "Stop... Really!?"
"Ummmm... Really. Rumidi wants to meet you... :^)"

Rumidi is not very old, 24-25 years. She is almost friendly. After Rumidi came on the first day, I took the Facebook ID Name from Hiya. Talked to her on the messenger, I realised that Rumidi might love me and be a good friend here. That's when I talked to her and realised that she is just like us— There is no such thing as arrogance or bigotry.

I said, "All right. But where will we meet?"

"Heyyyy bro!!! I'm Rumidi. I took her phone from her to talk to you... Please don't mind" I realised that Rumidi had been by Hiya's side for so long. And now she's talking to me.

"Yeah-yeah... It's ok... Please tell"

"I mean, brother, do you have a garden in front of your house?"

I said, "Yeah, Mmm... There is. There is also a small park. There is a river behind it again."

Rumidi said, "Can we go for a walk there?"

"Yeah... Of course. Come on in, take a look and enjoy yourself!"

"Well, that's fine, though."

"Come in the afternoon, it will be good to see. Otherwise, there is a lot of sunlight's heat at noon, it will be uncomfortable."

"OK (◔‿◔)"

The next day I was very excited. They are coming in front of my house. And bigger than that, Hiya is coming.

My parents are sleeping in the house, this opportunity. Today I wear her favourite t-shirt, orange. I got ready and left the house. I took out the phone and checked the message and saw that they had left. Inside the park.

As soon as I entered, I saw Hiya's face first. I saw Rumidi standing behind her. I started talking to her,

"Hey! Nice to meet you..."

Hiya introduced me, "You see the one sitting there, she is my Older sister— 'Mejdi'." I looked up and saw that Risha had come with them.

After talking for a while, Rumidi said, "You guys talk. I'm coming from a little side."

I went to one side and sat in a place like a round concrete bench. Hiya did not sit next to me then. Was standing in front. I said,

"Sit down. You have been standing since then. Today I see you are ashamed."

Hiya said, "No, no not actually..."

"Then?"

"Take a picture? I wear your favourite T-shirt.

"OK, Click up..."

We took a lot of pictures. I also took a lot of pictures with Rumidi, Mejdi and Hiya. Hiya and I were sitting on the big swing, Rumidi took the video again. After that, we went, to the river bank and took pictures together.

I put them forward. Rumidi bought ice cream for all of us. When it was time for them to return home. I said,

"Goodbye! Come to our park again." Rumidi & I shook hands and said.

Hiya raised her hand and said, "High-Five!"

I also did a high-five with her. And, that was her first touch.

5

Touch of An Unrequited Love

When Hiya came with her sisters that day, her sister told me a lot even though Hiya was hiding. I will tell my readers now, that I have never told Hiya. Rumidi told me behind Hiya that day,
"I have read many of your poems. Who are you writing about?"
I laughed and said, "No, no. Not with anyone, that's how I write!"
"Tell me the truth! Promise me to tell you the truth?"
"I do not promise..." I said something could guess.
"Oh, all right... Forget then..."
"Say, say, listen"
"Promise yourself first!"
"Well, Promise. Don't tell anyone?" After keeping quiet for a while, I said to Rumidi again,
"I love Hiya. I don't know when it turned from friendship to love..."
"That's what I wanted to hear from you. You didn't say that to Hiya, did you?"

I said, "No... I heard it in her one day, it was her family problem. Second, I have to be five or six years older than her. Third, she wants the boy to have a government job, to have a fair complexion, and finally to be liked by her parents..."

Rumidi said, "If you never misbehave with my sister, if you can make yourself perfect for Hiya, then I'm always on the side for your...

I'm by your side because I also like you as my brother...

I mean, I thought I'd see my sister's husband."

Rumidi, in the light of my first words, began to say again, "My sister is a little immature. That's why I never listen to her words. And in just a few days, I've come to understand that you love my sister."

I kept shut in silence. Rumidi said again,

"Listen! Mimi's would-be husband that you know about the images, that's my aunt's intelligence...

They still think nothing of it. If you stay by her side to persuade her aunt to stay with her till the end, then she will surely be able to fix everything.

Do you know another thing, brother? People who are always by one's side, they live very kindly, they are very good. Always loves to help."

I didn't say anything and said, "Um-mm... Yes!"

"And now she takes most of your words casually because you are still his friend, good friend. So like all friends, Hiya same treats you too. Become a best friend, then slowly tell her everything, one day all will be okay..."

I have known Rumidi for so long. But one thing is for sure, Rumidi became very good in my eyes, even if there is a slight difference between good and very good. I don't think I've ever received so much support, so much love, from anyone before. Even if she assures me that she is the sister of the one I love, she is very happy inside.

Remember, it's easy to feel Like, but Love is very difficult. In true love, the word 'I love you' does not become clear with the mouth. But every time you say 'I love you' in your mind by the name of the person you are going to love from behind.

Hiya and I would have tuition at the same time on Monday morning. Moreover, we started meeting some days. Hiya would go to Sanskrit tuition on Monday afternoon, I would meet there. She would go to Bengali tuition on Wednesdays and Fridays, and we started meeting there too.

April 1st, April Fool's Day. Suddenly, two days before, she was telling me on WhatsApp,

"What are your plans for April Fool's Day???"

I said, "Do you have to make a fool of yourself by planning again on April Fool's Day?"

Hiya laughed a little and said, "Yes, it is, it is very... If you want to make a big fool, you have to plan..."

I said, "Okay! But what is your plan?"

Hia typed something long and wrote,

"I plan that on April Fool's Day, we will both get status together... And people will respond by seeing that, and in response, we will fool them... (◠‿・)—☆"

"Really... What a plan! Huh"

"Today is Friday... Will you come to meet me?"

"Yes, I will. After the tuition? Right?"

"Umm... Then we will take pictures with both hands at the same time... All right? I'll give it status, then..." Laughing.

"Are you serious? Will you take a picture with me holding hands?" I couldn't believe it, Hiya was telling me to hold her hand.

Hiya said, "Have I ever lied to you before?? You tell yourself... If you come today, we will take pictures... Now I have to go for a bath, bye..."

"Well, that's fine. Bye!"

Leaving the house, I went to Hiya. She finished her tuition class and stood beside me. I said again,

"Will you take pictures?" I still can't believe it.

Hiya didn't say much and said bluntly, "Give me your hand."

I straightened my hand with a little fear in front of her. She took out his mobile phone and leaned over me and gave me her cool hand. For a few seconds, my hair seemed to tremble. I held her hands tightly inside me. I didn't like her pictures so I started clicking a few more random ones. Hiya was wearing a bracelet watch in her hand. I was still drowning in the touch of her hand.

Is this just a touch of friendship? Or, is there a touch of love hidden somewhere in it? To me, it's a 'Touch of An Unrequited Love'. Many times I read different novels and saw different movies, but like us, I could not find any part of this story anywhere.

What can we name this story? Can I just say, 'Don't Leave Me?' with just a drop or two of tears?

6

Middle Level Between Friendship and Relationship

The surprise I got on April Fool's Day was unexpected. We then planned to go out to meet one day. Hiya bunked her tuition to meet me that day— we sat by a lake and talked for about an hour and a half.

Then one more day we went out of the shopping mall and took pictures of the two of us.

Risha took pictures of us together. We both held each other's hands then. We walked down the street at the same time many times, many times we held each other's hands.

One day, Hiya unknowingly saved me from being hit by a car in the back. Is it our love for each other? Or something else? So I once said very emotionally,

"Hiya? Is our relationship a 'Middle Level Between Friendship and Relationship'?"

Hiya replied, "Maybe yes, maybe not! ಥ_ಥ"

I ask myself many times, is the relationship between us one kind of friendship? Or a secret love affair?

Many boys have proposed in her life And I looking for the answer to this question. Many boys have flirted with Hiya. But Hiya never went astray. Didn't want to leave me. Two or three girls proposed to me, and I declined them all. I don't want to lose that Hiya, I don't want to leave her.

But the situation dragged us down. Her father has seen a good boy for her. For that, Hiya is not allowed to roam with anyone and is not allowed to talk to anyone.

Hiya's own didi's husband's house, her marriage has been fixed. Hiya told me the whole story one afternoon.

I don't know how much is true and how much is false. But hearing these words in her mouth, I was quite stunned for a while. There were tears in my eyes, but I didn't let Hiya understand. I just wanted her to always be happy. I don't like to see the impression of depression on her face. Because, there is only one person who has made me laugh in my life— if she was not in my life, I would not have understood how big the distance of love is. I could not open my heart and smile. The contribution that Hiya has made to my life may never be forgotten.

I don't know if I can get Hiya again like before. That's all I told her that afternoon,

"You don't have any more relationship with me... Stay well, take care of yourself... You are getting thinner and thinner day by day!! I like to see you eat and drink well... Goodbye, Hiya!"

With this, I deleted my WhatsApp. I cried out loud in her absence. But I didn't let anyone know, no one understood, and no one listened.

Even as I write this, tears well up in my eyes. You may think while reading these, these stories are somewhat false. But no, that's the real thing, the real story. I still spend every day alone. I can still see Hiya in my dreams every night today, and no one from the side should say, 'Don't Leave Me'...

7

Thoughts of Rahul and Shyam

“Rahul, are you ready? But we have to get out this time” said Shyam, tying his shoelaces.
“Yeah, I'm coming...” Rahul came out of the bathroom wiping his wet hair.

Hanging the towel on the iron grill. The hairs on his head were moving with his hands. He put on his jeans. Rahul came out after spraying perfume with the buttons of his shirt.

Shyam was sitting on the bike outside waiting. Coming from behind, Rahul said,
“All right, let's go now.”

Shyam was riding his bike and Rahul was sitting in the back. As he ride, Shyam asked,
“Hey! Listen? Did you bring his card? If we have to go and stand there if we see... Our friend's program... And we can't get in...”
Rahul put his hand on Shyam's shoulder and said with a smile, “Hey, don't worry, that's all. Our childhood friend has reached such a big place today, so will he forget us now?

Even if we forget to bring the card, he will Manage it."
"You are right. He is such a great! He has grown so big, but there is no arrogance in him... Can you imagine!"
"Hmm... But it must be said that he is a very simple boy. And because of his simplicity, everyone loves him and the boy suffers a lot... Almost every moment..."
"Whatever... We can't even get into his personal affairs now, can we? When we were teens, we used to share everything, then we were young, it was accepted. And now he has enough respect!"

Rahul started saying, "Shyam have you ever thought?"
"What?"
"You were talking about his respect! Aren't you?
Ever thought we would make this boy so respected? Everyone at school trolled him... Laughter and jokes about him continued all the time. Even everyone blamed him and treated him well."
"It simply came to our notice then. The boy who could not do anything in school, and he is in such a big place today... But he never failed. Passed with low marks, never failed the exams although."
"Oh, Come on! We're glad he's in such a good place now. Or?"
"Mm-hmm... Yeah, that's it."

It's been almost many years since they left school. Sometimes they had no relationship with anyone. Someone has gone out to study, so someone has gone to different places for a job again.

Rahul and Shyam are now working in a private company in Bangalore— Both are engineers. They have been friends for about fifteen years. They studied together from their childhood and got a job in the same place. Although private companies, how long will not stay!

Their friend's program is going to see about ninety-three miles of road biking. Sometimes Rahul is riding the bike once and Shyam is riding again. Laughing and joking, the two of them crossed the road and finally reached the front of the auditorium.

8

The Girl in The Yellow Saree

Book posters all around— 'Don't Leave Me'. A large poster in front of the gate reads, "Welcome Best Selling Author, Ayan Dutt"

Leaving the bike in the parking zone, two friends entered showing their cards. Huge big hall. There are posters of Ayan's book and some pictures of him in big pictures all around.

Shyam was looking around like a strange man. Suddenly he shook Rahul's neck and said,

"Look over there, brother, Srikantada is sitting."

"Where are you talking about?"

"Come with me, let's see if we can talk to him!"

Shyam got up from behind and stood in front of the seat. Srikanta and a lady were laughing and talking. Shyam came between them with folded hands and said,

"Hello, sir! We are a big fan of yours. Can we get your autograph?"

Srikanta laughed and said, "Yeah! Of course."

Shyam and Rahul both took out a notepad and gave it to him. Rahul said,
"Sir! But your last novel was great. Tears welled up in my eyes as I read the last part."
Srikanta took the pen out of his chest pocket and said,
"Thanks! Ayan is also a good writer of the story 'Don't Leave Me'. It is different to tell a whole life story in a short story. Not everyone can write like him..."
Shyam said, "Yes sir. The boy has a lot of talent!"
Srikanta asked with a look of surprise, "Do you know him or not?"
Shyam said, "Of course, he is our childhood friend. We all went to high school together. Then he went to the arts stream, and we went to science."
Srikanta laughed and said, "Hey, is he your friend? You have to tell me first. Ahh! You guys..."
"No, I Mean... Actually..." Rahul muttered.
"Anyways, sit here," Srikanta said.

Shyam stared in surprise. He couldn't believe he was sitting next to her favourite author. They both thanked Ayan silently.

"You see, Shyam, what a reputation Ayan has become. How many wise people have come today. How many writers, reporters." They sat on the sofa.
Shyam whispered, "We're sitting next to such a great writer, have you noticed?"
"Yes, that's right. He is sitting next to us today, can you imagine?"

Coffee shop on one side of the auditorium. A beautiful girl is sitting there. Long heel shoes, a beautiful yellow saree on her body, a necklace designed around the neck, light earrings in the ears, and hair spread evenly. With light kajal in her eyes and dark lipstick on her lips, she sipped on the coffee cup.

The girl is sitting alone outside the auditorium stage drinking coffee. A boy and a girl came and stood in front of her. The boy said,

"How are you Hiya?"

"I am just fine. How are you?" Hiya stood up and said.

The girl replied, "We are fine too. Today is such a big event for Shreyas's best friend, Shreyas may not have come again!" The girl started laughing.

"Yes..." Hiya said again— "But I saw you again after a long time. Well Jyoti, are you in Delhi now?"

"Yes... Do you know? What pressure from the office... I rarely came home on vacation, and Shreyas brought me here." Jyoti looked at Shreyas and said.

Hiya— "No, no, you did it right. Come on! Watch his show, it will be good. Besides, Shreyas is there."

"You're looking at it this way!" But I did not force you at all. You wanted to come too." Shreyas frowned.

Hiya said to calm them down, "Hey, it's done... Please stop now... One of your nights is wasted! Whatever it is!"

Shreyas Ayan's best friend. They have been friends for almost twenty years. Shreyas, like Ayan, loves to be very simple, always smiling. When Shreyas falls in Class XI, he falls in love with the light of Class Twelve. And since then, their love affair continues to develop.

The top of the stage is decorated with various posters of the book 'Don't Leave Me'. There are some table leaves in front, chairs arranged behind it. On the left side of the stage is a beautifully arranged mic for the writer. The reporters are sitting in the lower chairs, the lights men are sitting on one side.

"Well, Shyam, do call Shreyas once! See when he will come" Rahul told Shreyas to call.

Shyam took the phone out of his pants pocket and called Shreyas‘ number. Said,
“Hello Shreyas, where are you? We are waiting for you.”

Shreyas gestured to Hiya and Jyoti and said,
“Come on now, they are calling...”
He said on the phone, “Yeah, we are right next to the coffee shop. You sit there, we are coming.”
“All right, come on.” That said, Shyam put the phone in his pocket.

Hiya left the cup of coffee on the table and went in front of the stage with Shreyas and Jyoti.
Shreyas grabbed Jyoti’s shoulder and came in front of Rahul and Shyam and said,
“Here we are. And this girl is my future wife.” He pulled one side of her cheek and smiled.
Jyoti removes Shreyas’ hand from her cheek and says “Huh...!” Said and sat down.
“The girl behind you...!?” Shyam got stuck trying to say something.
“Hiya, right?” Rahul said looking at her.
She stood back and said, “Yes.”
Shreyas— “And since you have seen her in WhatsApp status of Ayan before. So, today you could not recognise her. No?”
Hiya laughed and said, “Ayan used to talk about you. But we never met.” Hiya said laughing.
“And finally we met today, yes?” Rahul said.
“Yeah... Finally” said Hiya.

9

Book Is a Kind of Emotions

"Hello ladies and gentlemen, good evening. I am Ayan Dutt, one of your favourite writers.

Over the last two or three years, you have been appealing to me for the opportunity to talk to you face to face, or to come live from a social site. But I'm sorry, I couldn't keep up with your request." Ayan started saying the words in front of everyone with his hand on the microphone of the stage. A huge crowd has been gathering at the bottom of the stage so far since Ayan started his speech. As the reporter's powerful flashlights caught the eye of various dignitaries sitting on the stage, Ayan continued his speech

"It simply came to our notice then. The way I have been restless for these few months, this one year, it is hard to say." After a moment of silence, Ayan said again—

"It simply came to our notice then. And that's why I couldn't communicate with you. I always started to stay at home, I also forgot about the outside environment.

Two or three friends would visit from time to time. They used to say,

'Once you bring yourself on social media, your fan-followers are growing day by day. You don't want to talk to us right now— you can't end your life for a girl. You have your own life, you have your future. And the biggest thing is— You're one of everyone's favourite writers. Have you ever thought? How much respect you have when you go out!'

My friends have inspired me in many ways during that time. They explain that life never stops...

Slowly returning to normal life. Then comes the invitation to attend various events; Ignoring everything, so I am in front of you today." He leaned back a little and drank a sip of water.

Coming in front of the mic, Ayan was going to say something again. A girl stood up from behind. The tone of the question in her throat— Se said,

"Sir, what exactly happened to you? And why have you been depressed for so long?"

After asking the girl two questions, the noise of the audience seemed to stop. Someone is saying,

"What happened to you?"

Again, "Is the story of 'Don't Leave Me' really about all the events in your own life?" The interest in the audience continues to grow.

Ayan says with his face in front of Mic,

"I will say everything. I will try to answer every word, every question. Please don't be restless. I will tell you everything one by one."

Everyone sat in their chairs. Reporters' camera flashes were repeatedly reflected in Ayan's eyes. He looked at the audience and said,

"The only question you all have in mind is whether the 'Don't Leave Me' story is based on my own real life!

I am usually less active on social media. However, when I turn them on, this is the only question that comes up among you.

When I came out of the house today, I remembered a lot before coming here—

Well, have you ever wondered? People love to watch movies, even though most people understand nothing but movies. They just love to see different pictures in front of their eyes, But they never think about who wrote the whole story of the movie, and who arranged the stories inside the movie.

I know, many may ask me, will we stop watching movies? Do we know just by reading books? If this is the question, then my answer is 'No'.

There are more movie lovers than book lovers in this age. They think, ah! I have to read such a big novel, damn it! It's better to watch movies! It will also save time, and all the colourful pictures will come to the fore.

I know that It takes a long time to read a book or a novel and at the same time it requires patience. But look, I don't know if there is anything greater than the characters that are presented through imagination after reading the book...

However, I would like to say this one last thing to the movie lovers, that, why not watch a movie, you must watch it. Try more... The original story of some movies is never found in a book... Watch those movies, and notice the name of the writer at least once. Think about him, how he presented a beautiful story in the form of a movie.

Do you know a word? I have been wanting to direct movies for a long time. My father's condition was not good when I wanted to go out and study after giving 12. I couldn't— because it's not my fault, it's my father's.

Yes! My father's fault was that he could not go out and study me. Don't speak?

'It was my father's fault that my father was born in a poor house, but it is my fault if I die poor at the time of death.'

So I could not go out and read at that time. I was upset for a couple of months, but slowly I realised.

And I've been holding my pen ever since it doesn't take much money to write! So I started writing, I used to write poems and stories based on what I saw.

We belong to a middle-class family. My dad has a small business that he runs and manages four people. Just like when we go to the front of the movie screen— Just like a movie director presents the whole movie to the audience, in the same way, the head of the family or the father of all of us puts their good and bad away, they try to reach a good place...

And that's why today standing on this stage, I can say the words... I have published a book, I can slowly fulfil my dreams. The character of moral education given by my father behind this success is truly undeniable.

I don't know if directing my movie will ever be complete! But yes! Even if I can't manage, my writing will never stop until the end of my life."

The sound of applause could be heard in the distance. Hiya looked at Ayan with one glance and listened.

Ayan said, "I want to tell my teenager siblings that you read books— Read more books. Why not watch a movie, watch— But very few. It's not your age to watch movies. If you become interested in movies from this age, you will no longer want to read books when you grow up.

So I say, start reading more books now.

Remember, reading a book is a kind of emotion— If you fall in love with it, sometimes you will smile, sometimes you will shed tears..."

After a long time, a smile appeared on Ayan's face with the loud cheers and applause of the audience.

10

I Forgot Her

Ayan walks together with his sorrows at every step. He never said out loud that he wanted it, he wanted it! His loved ones have hurt him a lot— The ones he thought were his own have dropped bombs on him from behind.

As soon as the audience stopped cheering, Ayan started saying,

"My Cousin! I can't reveal her name; I would like to highlight a few things in front of you today...

Even if they do watch this TV show, I still have nothing to do— Because I think it's a good idea to put these things in front of you... You can tell, was I wrong then!

I have wanted to read books since I was very young. I never thought I would be a writer when I grew up. Whatever it was, I read different books as well as did some writing. My early writings, however, are about poetry; Later I started writing short stories.

When I was in Class 11 or, 12. One day my Cousin told me all the events of her life in one night. I listened to her, as usual, that day.

What a day was! I suddenly thought that a lot of short stories have been written, this time a book can be

11

I Missed You

Hiya had been sitting on the stage with her friends for so long. On hearing Ayan's call 'Miss Chatterjee', her heart throbbed. Hiya got up from the chair and slowly started walking towards the stairs of the stage.

Ayan went to the front of the stairs and extended his hand toward Hiya. Hiya got up on stage holding his hand, standing next to Ayan's mic.

"Dear viewers! Standing next to me, I hope you can't wait to name her.
This is Hiya— Hiya Chatterjee."

There was a great deal of excitement in the audience. Many are heard to say,
Who is this girl? Is this Real Hiya? Whose story did we find in 'Don't Leave Me'?

The conversations between the spectators began to float in Ayan's ears. He snatched their words and put his face in front of Mic and said,
"Yes, you are right— This is Hiya. Whose words were found in the story 'Don't Leave Me'. Ayan put his hand on her shoulder. Ayan gestured for Hiya to say something about herself in front of the audience.

"Good evening! People. I am Hiya Chatterjee. I'm studying final year in MA with Philosophy honours.

So far, I have not been able to say anything new that in the story written by Ayan, I have found a place in the role of the main Heroine.

I never thought anyone could write about me! I never really thought... When I read his book, all the moments seemed to coincide with us from the first meeting to the last journey. Could not help but wonder what was wrong with Ayan." As soon as she remembered her thoughts, tears came to her eyes. She looked at Ayan and said,

"I missed you Ayan, I missed you!" Hiya came over to Ayan's chest and hugged him.

Tears in the eyes of both of them. Both of them are hugging each other standing on that stage in front of people from all over the world as if they are presenting themselves today...

Wiping away the tears, he turned around in front of the stage. Ayan took her hand by the side of the hair and held it in her hand and raised it long, in front of the audience. Ayan said with his face in front of the mic,

"What are you thinking? Is the 'Don't Leave Me' story, however, happily ever after? Has Ayan Dutt been able to tell Hiya Chatterjee the words of his mind?" Ayan put the words in front of the audience with various questions.

The audience remained silent. Ayan said to himself,

"No! We are not couples, we are just friends. Each other's best friends. The feeling of my previous love for Hiya seems to have died somewhere. Now she's just a good friend of mine, and I'm a good friend of hers... Nothing more than that."

The whole room seemed to be buzzing with applause from the audience. Ayan came down from the stage with some of his last speeches.

Ayan came to the green room and sat in a chair. He also asked Hiya to sit next to him.

Ayan— "How are you now?"

Hiya— "I'm OK. But suddenly?" Ayan's strange question seemed to make Hiya think a little.

"Just OK?" He Muttered. "I've been calling you for two weeks to come to this show. Finally, I told Shreyas to make arrangements to communicate with you. If he hadn't helped, you probably wouldn't be here today."

"You have such a big event, and I can not come to know?" Said with a little laugh. "Do you know what happened?

I changed my number, about a month ago. And the pressure that I was under admission, these few days! So there was no time to tell you the new number."

It was as if a small blow came into Ayan's mind. Leaving it secret, he smiled and said,

"You will be busy now— You will go out to visit different places, you will eat and drink good and bad— And I! I'm just yours...

Anyways! How is Soumya?"

Soumya is the groom to be here. Her father had a relationship with him a long time ago. When Ayan was in Class 12, he knew a little about the man.

Ayan had no relationship with Hiya for about five years. When Ayan left Hiya when she was in class 12, she told Ayan a lot and tried to explain a lot, but she failed.

Hiya also told Ayan, 'Please don't leave me... Please... I will be very lonely... Please! My best friend and you, I have no one but you two. Please don't leave me.' Who cares, then!

There is no question of losing love— Even their friendship was ruined in the middle. Judging by that, the fault of Ayan was the biggest. When he had deliberately left Hiya alone, he should not have left her that way. Who is to say that maybe the same feeling towards Hiya was born then!

He shouldn't have let Hiya go. He should have been by Hiya's side and stood by her bad times. But he couldn't— just put a small mistake in the heat of anger, so maybe she's someone else today!

'One hand does not clap'— She could have brought her back in a day or two. But Hiya was stubborn, she also turned around and did not say anything— Did not say that,

Ayan! Please don't do this to me, never ruin your friendship with me. Come back to the previous again...

This may have happened due to a misunderstanding between the two of them. On the other hand, Hiya started coming and started forgetting Ayan. Meanwhile, Ayan Hiya's memory slowly began to go into depression.

Hiya began to forget him, hanging out with her father's favourite boy. On the other hand, Ayan started writing novels about her...

Hiya sipped her cold drink glass and said,

"Soumya? He is somehow leaving— He is still in Calcutta."

"Does he have a job?"

"No, he left the job two months ago. Now he is just applying here and there in search of a good job"

Ayan smiled with fake. He said, "He must get it." He didn't let Hia understand anything else.

Shyam slapped him twice on the neck and said, “We are by your side, brother. You will never stop writing. No matter how many storms come, you will continue to twist them.”

Before getting into the Auto, Jyoti hugged Shreyas and said ‘good night’.

Rahul and Shyam rode their bikes toward the hotel.

The driver brought the car and parked it in front of Ayan. Shreyas said, “I am sitting in the front seat. You guys sit back.”

Car is running— Shreyas is sitting in front and scrolling Facebook on his mobile. Sitting in the back, Ayan is looking at the distant road through the glass of the car. Hiya’s eyes are once out of the glass, again rolling towards Ayan’s face. She wants to say something but sits quietly.

Hiya put her head on Ayan’s shoulder. Ayan put his hand on Hiya’s head and began to speak through her hair. Said, “What happened to Miss Chatterjee? Don’t you have a good mood?” Shreyas glanced through the car mirror and looked at his mobile again.

Ever since Ayan was in Class 11, he has been calling her ‘Miss Chatterjee’. One day while talking on WhatsApp, Ayan suddenly said,

“Your name... It doesn’t look good on my mobile! These four letters seem to be very small— H, I, Y, A. I thought of a good name for you, listen?”

Hiya replied with a few smiley emoticons, “I will listen. My friend has chosen such a beautiful name, I can not hear? (◔‿◔)”

Ayan wrote, “How is the name of ‘Miss Chatterjee’?
I thought I would save your contact name with it.”

“Oh Gosh! You are a genius. Someone can call me by such a beautiful name! The more I think about you, the more I feel proud. You write such beautiful stories and poems. You have a lot of talent! My life is really happy, having a friend like you!" Hiya replied.

Ayan said, "Hey, why? Do you just talk to me to compliment me? That is why I am very angry. Why are you always looking for my talent! Well look, do you have less talent? You are so beautiful in your studies, you look so beautiful— You are an expert in housework. And what I like most is how beautiful you are acting! Who can do this acting?

God sends in everyone from birth with some of the other talents, who use them properly to become a good person. Again, someone or something abuses it."

Hiya seemed to have gone somewhere in her thoughts. Hiya came back to the present after shaking twice.

Ayan slowly lifted Hiya's head off his shoulder with his hand and said,

"Shreyas has come home."

Shreyas landed in front of his house. Hiya said from inside the car, "If you go to our site, you will come to our house, okay?"

Shreyas said, "Okay!" His hand reached out to Ayan, saying "Never give up!"

Ayan said at the same time with a smile, "Never give up!"

"Okay, bye guys... Good night." Shreyas walked towards the door of his house.

"Good night." Ayan closed the car door and said.

"Are you staying in my flat today? Even though it's night, it's impossible to go that far." Ayan said looking at Hiya.

Hiya said, "Mm-hmm! I thought I'd stay in your flat tonight. Because it will be late at night, going home."

She placed her hand on the hand resting on Ayan's leg. Ayan looked at her and hugged her.

Hiya whispered in Ayan's ear, "I really miss you so much!"

Ayan also said, “I miss you too!”

13

They Kissed Each Other

He got up from the elevator and stopped on the second floor. Hiya said,

"I will probably enter your flat in three or four months. Even though I met you after so long. The last time I saw you were in this flat."

Hiya came to visit Ayan's flat with Soumya at that time. Although not for long, they were gone for a short time.

Ayan occasionally brings himself in Soumya's place. Thinks, if he could have been himself instead of Soumya! Hiya might have always been happy... But, there is no point in thinking about that anymore— Ayan has lost that place due to his own mistake.

When Ayan says occasionally, how is Soumya? Where is the Soumya? —His own throat gets stuck while talking. He doesn't want to say it, but he has no choice. Because, no matter what, he's a good friend. He should take the news of good and bad, happiness and sorrow.

When she answers Ayan's question, she says he's fine— Or something else... Then Ayan realises that something is stuck somewhere inside her throat, just like him. Ayan does not say all that publicly, lest she what think! Or, even if their friendship breaks down again!

Soumya had earlier agreed with Hiya that "Our relationship is with us. But never speak in such a way that Ayan and my friendship is ruined... You have been here for some time in my life, but Ayan has understood me. He gives me enough dignity and respect. And if I could not give any importance to him, then what is this friendship!

That's why I told you before so that you don't come into our friendship..."

Soumya is such a good boy, quite calm. Short hair and his humble attitude can be seen in his speech and demeanour. Although Ayan is occasionally angry with Soumya, very little. He doesn't seem to be talking to him, he's Hiya's future groom. It was as if two friends were sitting together talking. Sometimes Ayan thinks,

'Soumya does such a good job... He has a car, he has a house, and what else does it take... Bigger than that— He is a Brahmin, a favourite boy of Hiya's parents...

I could never be their son-in-law— Though, that's normal!

It may have been written in destiny.'

Hiya's agreement with Soumya's was quite agreeable though. He also does not want Hiya to be unhappy at any time— Let the stream of sorrow come down in her. So, whenever Hiya wanted, she would meet Ayan. Even in the middle of the night, if she heard of any danger to Ayan, she would run away.

Opening the door key, Ayan said, "Give me your bag. Come inside."

Hiya closed the door with her shoes inside. Said, "Ayan! I'm going to freshen up first, then see if anything can be made!"

Ayan looked at the kitchen. He looked at the clock and saw that it was half-past eleven.

Ayan's parents left home four days ago. Ayan's sister Rumi's final exam a few days later. So now his parents will be with Rumi for a month.

It's been three years since Ayan's father bought the flat. Ayan also gave some of his savings and money from book sales. Later, the two of them bought the flat and decorated it well.

Besides, Ayan had already wanted to take a flat in Main Town. It was very difficult to get to and from various publishing houses from his house, he had to book hotels occasionally.

So he slowly made a plan and bought the flat.

Hiya came out of the bathroom with a wet face. She looked at Ayan and wiped his face and said,

"Go and wash your face-hands and take rest, I will make something..."

Hiya entered the kitchen and boiled the Chowmein. Ayan went in front of her and put his hand on her shoulder and said,

"Hello, Chef! Are you making Chowmein for me?"

"Yes! Mr Writer"

After a while, she took Chowmein's plate in both hands and placed it in front of Ayan. Ayan said,

"Slowly! Be careful"

Ayan turned on the TV. He said to Hiya,

"Will you watch the movie?"

Hiya replied, "OK"

After a while, Ayan got up from the sofa and stood beside the fridge. He came to the sofa with the bottle of red wine kept inside the fridge and sat down again. Hiya is still watching movies at a glance.

As he straightened the wine glasses on the table, Ayan asked, "Drink?"

Hiya said, "Wine! Oh my gosh! Yeah... Of-course..."

He poured wine into the glass. He said to Hiya, "Well! You stay with me, won't there be any problem?"

Hiya took a sip from the glass and turned off the TV with the remote. Some of the body parts inside the Ayan became agitated due to this reaction of Hiya.

Hiya got up on Ayan's thighs— Facing his face, and spread her long hair evenly behind Ayan's head.

A glass of wine in both hands. Feelings of instability in the eyes of both of them. Hiya is sitting on Ayan's thighs. They were both excited with the last sip of wine in the glass. Hiya tied her fragrant hair with her hands and gently placed her red lips on Ayan's lips.

Gradually, the tension between the two began to increase— They began to undress. Ayan put her lips on Hiya's lips and took her in her arms and went to bed.

ppp

The table lamp is burning. The inside of the room is covered with yellow dim light. Hiya is lying with her head on Ayan's chest, Ayan is moving her hand over Hiya's head. There are white sheets spread over their naked bodies.

To them that this love, love is completely useless. Knowing they would never be together, they became physically bound.

Ayan raised her face and said, "Hiya! Is that our epic story?"

She laughed and said, "Are you thinking of writing a story again?"

Ayan said, "Yes! I want the whole world to know our story... I do not want to leave any doubt in their minds so that it is difficult for them to understand."

They started kissing each other gently on the lips.

Author's Note

When I write, a lot of things come up, and a lot of things are wrapped inside it like leaves. Every writer is asked why he writes. I never compare myself to them, because they are wise writers. And, I'm a little.

I imagined that my handwriting would one day be published. Readers will one day be able to read my book and understand my thoughts, a dream I occasionally had.

My first written story was 'Shoksangbad', which I wrote when I was 16 years old. Then suddenly the tendency to write poetry came. I used to keep a notebook of what I wrote in my poems. I still do this today, keeping my inner mind in a notebook that I can't tell anyone.

The idea that I write for money is completely wrong. My writing is a kind of intoxication. And this intoxication once turned into love in me. I write to express the misery of human life, the love between them, and the burning of their heart. No money is needed to write— just a pen and paper is enough. And I am really glad that my manuscript from this paper-pen has been printed in the book today. However, Manik Bandyopadhyay said in one of his essays, "The author is merely a penman. If penmanship is of no use to him, then his life is much more meaningless and his survival is in vain than the work of a labourer sitting by the side of the road."

I was very worried about the publication of the book 'Don't Leave Me! I need you'. Today when I was able to bring the book in front of the readers, I feel very good.

First of all, I would like to thank Notion Press for carefully publishing my story. Dear readers, I hope the story of this book will be well received.

Editor's Note

Sayan Banik wrote his new book 'Don't Leave Me! I need you', based on a Bengali book. The English translation of this book is from the first story of his first Bengali book 'Chere Jeo Na'.

The book is mainly about one story, Hiya Chatterjee and Ayan Dutt. Here they bring to the fore many events of their school life and just then the road to the corner of their love begins. Will they be able to find their love? Will they really have a happy ending to their love, or will they leave each other?

As a narrator, Sayan Banik recounts Ayan's life story up to the sixth chapter of this book. The first story of his first book was written by Sayan Banik in these 6 chapters. He then proceeded to draw the end of this story with some more parts of it. As the saying goes, so does the work—he then added the last part of the story with seven more chapters.

Author's Bio

Sayan Banik was born in 2003 in West Bengal, India. Growing up, he was fascinated with the language 'Bengali' which eventually led to some early exposure to reading since he was clung to stories written in the language 'Bengali'. His inspiration is Ajay K Pandey who is an extremely popular English author of all times.

Sayan Banik pursued writing as his passion from a very young age during his school life when he first started writing short stories. Later, Sayan Banik, who had just passed the twelfth grade, developed a passion for the ideas. He expressed those in the number of stories he wrote which have been published in many weekly journals, one of those named 'Netphoring'. His talent and amiability soon won him great popularity among his readers and his stories are well loved by all till date.

In most of his stories, he explores the issue of how past events are unchangeable by introducing an ability to manipulate past events. He's best known for writing fictional books which have touched all his readers. Sayan Banik describes the trajectory of his background that culminates in his passion for ideas. He piques the curiosity of the reader as to how exactly one can manipulate past events.

In the book 'Don't leave me! I need you' he develops a sense of suspense, adding a touch of romanticism and perfectly maintains an emotional balance keeping the readers entertained and hooked right till the end.

9 798887 044903

Printed by Libri Plureos GmbH in Hamburg, Germany